W9-CKL-448

Task Time

The Sound of T

By Cynthia Klingel and Peg Ballard

The Child's World®

Task 1

Pitch the tent.

Task 2
Tilt the poles.

Task 3
Tap the stake.

Task 4
Tuck the flap.

Task 5
Catch some fish.

Task 6
Toss the fish into
the tub!

Task 7

Light the fire.

Task 8
Tip the pan.

Task 9
Fry some fish.

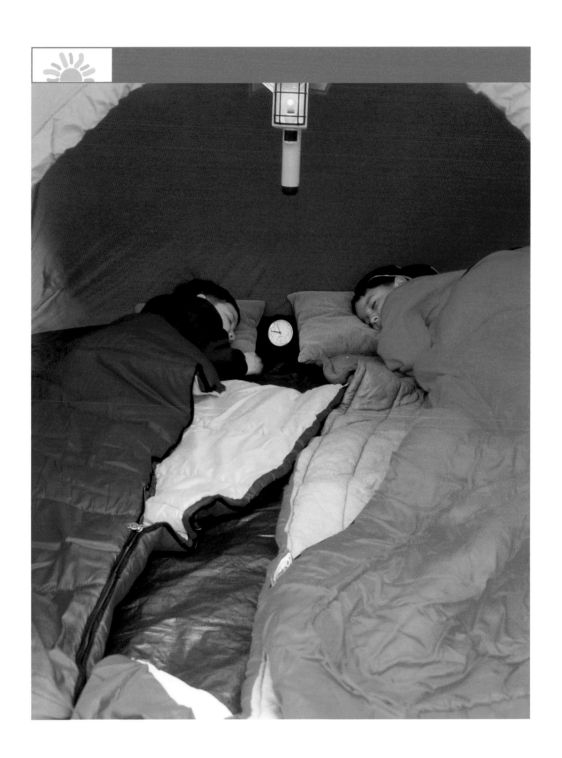

Task 10
Get to sleep by ten.

Word List

tap	tip
task	to
ten	toss
tent	tub
tilt	tuck

Note to Parents and Educators

Welcome to Wonder Books® Phonics Readers! These books are based on current research that supports the idea that our brains detect patterns rather than apply rules. This means that children learn to read more easily when they are taught the familiar spelling patterns found in English. As children progress in their reading, they can use these spelling patterns to figure out more complex words.

The Phonics Readers texts provide the opportunity to practice and apply knowledge of the sounds in natural language. The ten books on the long and short vowels introduce the sounds using familiar onsets and *rimes*, or spelling patterns, for reinforcement. The letter(s) before the vowel in a word are considered the onset. Changing the onset allows the consonant books in the series to maintain the practice and reinforcement of the rimes. The repeated use of a word or phrase reinforces the target sound.

As an example, the word "cat" might be used to present the short "a" sound, with the letter "c" being the onset and "–at" being the rime. This approach provides practice and reinforcement for the short "a" sound, since there are many familiar words with the "–at" rime.

The number on the spine of each book facilitates arranging the books in the order in which the sounds are learned. The books can also be arranged into groups of long vowels, short vowels, consonants, and blends. All the books in each grouping have their numbers printed in the same color on the spine. The books can be grouped and regrouped easily and quickly, depending on the teacher's needs.

The stories and accompanying photographs in this series are based on time-honored concepts in children's literature: Well-written, engaging texts and colorful, high-quality photographs combine to produce books that children want to read again and again.

Dr. Peg Ballard
Minnesota State University, Mankato, MN

About the Authors

Cynthia Klingel has worked as a high school English teacher and an elementary school teacher. She is currently the curriculum director for a Minnesota school district. Cynthia lives with her family in Mankato, Minnesota.

Dr. Peg Ballard holds a PhD from Purdue University and is an associate professor in the department of curriculum & instruction at Minnesota State University. Her area of expertise is diagnosis and remediation of reading difficulties. Dr. Ballard serves as a curriculum consultant and facilitator for school districts adopting new literacy programs. She has conducted in-service workshops and conference presentations on phonics instruction, literacy assessment and evaluation, and comprehension strategies.

Photo Credits

All photos © copyright: Romie Flanagan/Flanagan Publishing Services.
Cover: Romie Flanagan/Flanagan Publishing Services.

Special thanks to the Gnadt family

Photo Research: Alice Flanagan
Design and production: Herman Adler Design Group

Text copyright © 2000 by The Child's World®, Inc.
All rights reserved. No part of this book may be reproduced or utilized
in any form or by any means without written permission from the publisher.
Printed in the United States of America.

Library of Congress Cataloging-in-Publication Data

Klingel, Cynthia Fitterer.
    Task time : the sound of "t" / by Cynthia Klingel and Peg Ballard.
        p. cm. — (Wonder books)
    Summary : Simple text and repetition of the letter "t" help readers
learn how to use this sound.
    ISBN 1-56766-690-6 (lib. bdg. : alk. paper)
    [1. Alphabet.] I. Ballard, Peg. II. Title. III. Series: Wonder books
(Chanhassen, Minn.)
PZ7.K6798Tas   1999
[E]—dc21   99-25497
                                                       CIP

HLOOX   +
        E
        KLING

HOUSTON PUBLIC LIBRARY
DISCARDED

KLINGEL, CYNTHIA FITTERER.
TASK TIME

LOOSCAN
07/07